VIVIAN FRENCH

Illustrations by Colin West

WALKER BOOKS

AND SUBSIDIARIES

LONDON · BOSTON · SYDNEY

For dear Sarah Worm
with lots of love
V.F.

First published 1993 by
Walker Books Ltd, 87 Vauxhall Walk
London SE11 5HJ

This edition published 1995

4 6 8 10 9 7 5

Text © 1993 Vivian French
Illustrations © 1993 Colin West

This book has been typeset in Garamond.

Printed in England by Clays Ltd, St Ives plc

British Library Cataloguing in Publication Data
A catalogue record for this book
is available from the British Library.

ISBN 0-7445-3689-8

CONTENTS

THE IMPORTANT QUESTION

It was late summer, and everyone in the village of Nornigig was sitting in the square talking about the nearby village of Drumble Drone.

"Too clever by half, those old Drumblers," said Tom Coddy gloomily.

"That's right," said Sal Slinpole. "Too clever by half."

"Always thought as we were the cleverest," said Sammy Chuffinhead. "But now see what they've done. Put handles on their baskets, they have. Too clever by half."

Tom, Sal and Sammy all sighed
heavily, and so did all the other
villagers.

Little Mary Poggs was sitting
beside Tom Coddy, rubbing her chin.

"Why don't all of us Nornigigs build
a fine tall building to show those old
Drumblers how we're *much* the
cleverest?" she said.

There was a long silence. Tom Coddy scratched his ear, and asked Sal Slinpole. Sal asked Sammy Chuffinhead, and the idea went all round the village, and everyone nodded and said, "Arrrr". But then came the big question: *What shall we build?* And even Mary Poggs couldn't think of an answer.

"We must ask Old Down," Mary
said, and all the village agreed that
that was the thing they must do.

Now, Old Down was a thinker. He was long in his thinking, and slow, but everyone in the village knew that if you wanted the answer to a question you went to Old Down. You took a present with you and you were very polite and always said please, and told him what the problem was. After a day or two, or even a week or two if it was a difficult question, you went back with another present, and Old Down would tell you the answer.

Mary Poggs was very excited about going to see Old Down. It had been decided that this was such an important question that all the village should go, and every one of them was to bring a present. Mary thought hard, and decided on a bowl of ripe red apples.

She was rather disappointed
when she saw that everyone else
had had the same idea, but she
polished her apples until they
shone, and decorated them with
fresh green leaves.

OLD DOWN STARTS THINKING

All the villagers trailed slowly up the hill to Old Down's tower. Mary led the way, carefully carrying her bowl of shining apples.

Old Down was sitting outside his
tower in the sunshine. Mary waited
until the last small villager had
puffed his way up to the top of the
hill, and then presented her gift.
Old Down smiled.

"If you please, we all of us want to build a fine tall building," Mary said, "so we can show the Drumblers how clever we Nornigigs are. But we don't know what to build."

Old Down nodded. Each villager in turn placed his or her gift in front of him, and he watched the pile of apples grow higher and higher.

"No eggs or little soft cheesies?" he asked.

Mary Poggs thought he sounded rather peevish for such a wise old man, but she curtsied politely.

"When shall we come for the answer?" she asked.

"I'll be taking as long as I need," said Old Down, "but if there's one or two of you as wants to come along tomorrow, I'll see how it is with me. 'Tis a hard question, mind."

Mary curtsied again. "I'll be back tomorrow, and thank you ever so."

All the villagers followed her down the hill to their homes.

I'll be off to see Old Down early.

Mary went up the hill the next day with Tom Coddy for company. They took a basket of new laid eggs, and Old Down was cheerful.

"I'm thinking well," he said.

"Shall we come back tomorrow then?" Mary asked.

Old Down gazed at the sky. "Maybe the day after," he said.

Mary took Sal Slinpole with her on the next visit. Sal was carrying a bowl filled with soft cheese. Old Down smiled. "I'm thinking better and better. It's never been so quick to come before."

Old Down's so clever!

Mary clapped her hands. "You know what we can build?"

Old Down stopped smiling and sighed. "All of a rush, you little ones. 'Tis a hard question, and you must be patient."

Mary curtsied low. "I'm ever so sorry. We'll not come bothering you for a while."

She and Sal turned to go, but Old Down coughed.

"Maybe tomorrow … or the day after," he said. "Like I says, things is coming well."

"Thank you *ever* so," said Mary, and she and Sal skipped and hopped all the way down the hill to spread the good news.

THE ANSWER

Sammy Chuffinhead came looking for Mary a day or two later.

"Here's a fine chucky hen," he said. "Shall you take it to him up there to help him with his thinking?"

Mary thanked him. She tucked the hen under her arm and set off on her own up the hill.

Old Down was sitting outside his tower as usual.

He waved an arm at Mary and she put the hen down in front of him. It clucked, and began pottering about happily.

"The answer's nearly come." Old
Down spoke in a slow deep voice.

Mary gave a little gasp.

Old Down closed his eyes, and
Mary held her breath.

"Tell me the tallest building as
you can put your mind to." Old
Down sounded as if he was talking
in his sleep.

Mary shut her eyes, and thought hard. "My gran told me once of a tall church with a tall tower that tickled the sky."

Old Down let out a heavy sigh.

"Exactly so," he said. "Go and tell all of them down below."

A TALL tower, mind.

"Thank you *ever* so," said Mary, curtsying her best curtsy. "A tall church with a tall tower. I'll tell them – and they'll be as pleased as pleased could be. There's none of us could've thought of that." And she waved to Old Down and went hurrying off with the news.

The village of Nornigig had never
been so busy. Everyone was sawing
or chopping or chipping or
hammering or hauling baskets of
stones and planks of wood to the
centre of the market place where
the church was to stand.

31

"Those old Drumblers won't ever have anything as fine," Mary said proudly as the walls grew higher and higher.

32

Tom Coddy was too puffed to answer, but he nodded as he staggered past carrying a roof beam.

Up and up went the church. The walls were of wood and stones, and the roof and the tall tower were of wood. On the day the weathercock was put on the top of the tower a holiday was called.

"We should all go and sing in the church," said Mary Poggs. "And then we should have a great feast. And we should ask all the Drumblers to come along and see."

Everyone nodded.

Tom Coddy scratched his leg. "I'll be off to fetch them old Drumblers."

The villagers all lined up, with Mary at the front. Then the door of the church was flung open, and in they all marched. The smallest villager pulled the door shut behind him.

It was terribly dark.

None of them could see their hands in front of their faces.

"I think," said Mary Poggs, "that we forgot the windows."

"We did think to put in a fine big door," said Sal Slinpole.

"Where is it?" asked Sammy.

"Here," said Mary, and they all trooped out again.

BASKETS, BOWLS AND BUCKETS

They sat on the grass outside the church and stared at the walls.

"'Tis all your fault, Mary Poggs," said Sal. "You and your ideas. What'll those Drumblers say?"

"We ain't got time to ask Old
Down, neither," said Sammy. "Them
Drumblers will be here by sundown
or thereabouts – here to laugh, I
shouldn't wonder."

Mary was staring at the sky.
Suddenly she jumped to her feet.

"Quick! Bring all your baskets and bowls and buckets out here on the grass! We'll fill them full of sunshine, and then we'll tip it out in the church … and it'll be as bright as day!"

There was silence. All the villagers looked at Mary with their eyes and mouths wide open.

"Come on," said Mary.

Once again everyone began rushing to and fro. All the baskets and bowls and buckets were laid outside in the sunshine and left to

fill while the preparations for the feast went merrily on. Mary stood watch, and as the sun moved across the sky she turned the baskets so that no shade fell over them.

"Are they filled up?" Sammy asked, coming to peer in his basket.

"I reckon," said Mary. "We'd better start shutting the lids down and covering them over."

Sal and Sammy and Mary began to close up the baskets and cover over the buckets and bowls.

The other villagers came to watch, and Mary organized them into a line. "Carry them ever so carefully," she said. "No tripping or spilling or dropping."

Carefully, step by slow step, the sunshine was carried into the dark church.

"When I say *Now*," said Mary, "we'll let the sunshine out."

Everybody stood beside their bowl or bucket or basket, holding their breath.

"One, two, three – *now!*" Mary shouted.

There was a mighty rustling and rattling and clanging.

It was still terribly dark.

47

Mary shut her eyes very tightly. There was a sudden flash in her mind – a great flash of light.

"Of course!" she cried. "The sunshine's gone because the sun's gone down. It'll be here in the morning, sure as eggs is eggs."

"Of course it will," said the villagers, slapping each other on the back with relief. They picked up the baskets, buckets and bowls and carried them out of the church.

"Be sure and keep the door shut on that sunshine," said Mary. "Or there'll be none left tomorrow."

The smallest villager scuttled out quickly and slammed the door behind him.

"What about them Drumblers?" asked Sammy.

"Sun's gone down already," said Mary firmly. "And that door must be kept shut. They'll see our church and tower by moonlight ... no need for them to go inside."

MARY'S BRIGHT AND SHINING IDEA

Tom Coddy came hurrying into the
square. "Here we come... My, what
a sight for sore eyes that fine tall
church do be!"

A crowd of Drumblers was close behind him. There were loud cries of "*Oooooh!*" and "*Aaaaaah!*" as they saw the wonderful church.

"You Nornigigs do surely be the cleverest of folks round these here whichways," said their mayor, nodding his head over and over again.

The Nornigigs puffed up with
pride, and beamed at each other.
All, that is, except Mary Poggs.

Mary Poggs was hurrying up the
hillside towards Old Down's tower.

In one hand she carried a basket heaped high with good things from the feast, in the other a candle to light her way in the darkness.

"Old Down!" she called.

Old Down stretched, and yawned, and looked up from his excellent supper of apples and cheese and eggs.

"Old Down," Mary said, hurriedly
curtsying low. "Old Down, will
sunshine keep safe overnight?"

Old Down rubbed his nose
thoughtfully. "Ah," he said, "'tis a
difficult question."

Mary pushed the piled-up basket
of goodies into his arms.

"Please," she begged, "I need to
know terribly badly."

"'Tis too dark for thinking," Old Down said, peering into the basket. "I only think bright in the day, just like the sunshine. Bright as that there candle I am, come the day.

Could you shine that over here so's
I can see what you be a bringing?"

Mary Poggs took no
notice. She was
staring at the
candle, and
smiling. "Candles
can be as bright
as any sun," she
said to herself.

She jumped up.

"Thank you
ever so, Old
Down," she called
as she hurried off
down to the
celebrations.

57

Mary Poggs enjoyed the feasting,
and the singing, and the dancing.
She had slipped into the church with
fifty fine candles all ready for the
morning, and she made a note that
the stones in the wall under Tom
Coddy's roof beam were very loose.

"Might be a pretty place for a window," she thought to herself. And Mary Poggs knew that one day, when she was ready, she would find herself a tower on a hillside and sit in front of it and think.

"Old Poggs, they'll call me," she said to herself with a smile. "Wise Old Poggs."

And she skipped off to join in the dancing.

Drumble
drone

MORE WALKER SPRINTERS
For You to Enjoy

☐ 0-7445-3688-X   *Easy Peasy*
by Sarah Hayes/
John Bendall-Brunello   £3.50

☐ 0-7445-3686-3   *The Magic Boathouse*
by Sam Llewellyn/Arthur Robins   £3.50

☐ 0-7445-3666-9   *Beware the Killer Coat*
by Susan Gates/Josip Lizatovic   £3.50

☐ 0-7445-3687-1   *Hector the Rat*
by Tony Wilkinson   £3.50

☐ 0-7445-3664-2   *Gemma and the Beetle People*
by Enid Richemont/Tony Kenyon   £3.50

☐ 0-7445-3665-0   *The Biggest Birthday Card
in the World*
by Alison Morgan/Carolyn Dinan   £3.50

☐ 0-7445-3668-5   *Impossible Parents*
by Brian Patten/Arthur Robins   £3.50

Name _____

Address _____

_____